When I was a teacher, I was gifted the opportunity to see the world through the eyes of a child for over eight years. In that time, I saw the beauty in their spirits. Children understand that kindness is multifaceted. All kids want to do is live in a world in which we all are seen, loved, and valued for who we are. During my time in the classroom, I also realized how many children did not have access to books in their homes. I wanted to do something about it, which is why Kind Cotton was founded.

Kind Cotton is on a mission to put inclusive books into the hands of kids with every purchase. Our goal is to donate 1,000,000 books! The best part? Your purchase of *Kindness Is* gets us one step closer– we will be donating a copy to a child thanks to you!!!

♥ Kaitlin

Want to learn more?
Check out our website:

www.kindcotton.com

To my daughter and all the other children in the world.
May you always remember how to spread true kindness.
To my incredible partner, Kevin. Thank you for being the Jim to my Pam.

-K.J.

For my biggest little sis, Alexandra, who helped me get through the past year in more ways than she knows.
Love ya tons.

-F.L.

Kind Cotton, LLC
Silver Spring, MD

Book Design by Arlene Soto, Intricate Designs

Printed in the United States

Publisher's Cataloging-in-Publication
Provided by Cassidy Cataloguing Services, Inc.
Names: Johnstone, Kaitlin, 1986- author. | LeFevre, Felicity, 1976- illustrator.
Title: Kindness is / by Kaitlin Johnstone ; illustrated by Felicity LeFevre.
Description: Silver Spring, MD : Kind Cotton, LLC, [2023] | Audience: Kindergarten--3rd grade. | Summary: It's Kenzie's first day at a new elementary school. As she walks through the doors of her classroom, she begins to realize this school is unlike others she's been to. There aren't as many math and ABC charts. Instead, there are beautiful words, such as kindness and love painted throughout. Kenzie's teacher quickly gives them their first assignment: to write about what kindness means. With the help of her parents she proudly shares the true meaning of kindness with her peers. Kindness is love. Kindness is empathy. Kindness is compassion. Kindness is inclusion. Kindness is justice.--Publisher.
Identifiers: ISBN: 979-8-9886801-0-9 (Hardcover) | 979-8-9886801-1-6 (Paperback) | 979-8-9886801-2-3 (E-Book) | LCCN: 2023914807
Subjects: LCSH: Kindness--Juvenile fiction. | School children--Juvenile fiction. | Love in children--Juvenile fiction. | Empathy in children--Juvenile fiction. | Compassion in children--Juvenile fiction. | Fairness--Juvenile fiction. | Social integration--Juvenile fiction. | Children--Life skills guides--Juvenile fiction. | CYAC: Kindness--Fiction. | School children--Fiction. | Love-- Fiction. | Empathy--Fiction. | Compassion--Fiction. | Fairness--Fiction. | Belonging--Fiction. | Conduct of life--Fiction.
Classification: LCC: PZ7.1.J648 K56 2023 | DDC: [E]--dc23

Kindness Is

by Kaitlin Johnstone
illustrated by Felicity LeFevre

It was Kenzie's first day at Imagine Kind Elementary, and she could not wait to meet her new classmates.

Starting a new school was scary,
but her friend Angel was in her class,
which eased her worries.

Love
Kenzie
Mia

Walking through the
doors of her classroom,
she was greeted by her teacher,
Mr. Warner, who had a bright smile and a
purple tie that matched Kenzie's dress.
Just when she thought her new school could not get
any better, Mr. Warner explained that she could choose
to sit in any spot she'd like!

Be Kind

As she snuggled into a squishy unicorn pillow, she looked around and noticed the walls at this school were different. Instead of math and ABC charts, there were beautiful words, like *kindness* and *love* painted all around.

Wow, she thought to herself, **this place is magical.**

During circle time, Mr. Warner gave the class their first homework assignment. "I want to know what kindness means to you." Students eagerly raised their hands to brainstorm ideas.

"Holding the door for a friend," yelled Sydney.

"Writing your parents a card," said Maxi.

"Using your manners," whispered Manuel.

These are all beautiful examples, Kenzie thought as she stared at the paintings on Mr. Warner's walls, **but I feel like kindness is more.**

For the rest of the day, all she could think about was her homework. Her class visited the library and Kenzie looked through all the books she could find about kindness, but nothing she read felt just right.

During recess, she sat on a bench thinking while the other children played.

A few friends came over and asked her to join them in a game of soccer.

She knew it would be a good idea.
She needed a break from her homework assignment.

At dismissal, she raced to her mom to tell her all about her new school. After a few minutes of discussing the amazing tacos she ate for lunch, she eagerly asked, **"Momma, what is kindness?"** Her mom thought for a moment and replied, **"What is it to you?"**

STOP
love

love.
empathy.
Kindness
is

As soon as they arrived home, they sat on the couch with a notepad, Kenzie's fleece blanket, and a bowl of blueberries while they thought of some ideas.

Kenzie thought she'd never understand the true meaning of kindness, but she was determined not to give up. They talked and talked until Kenzie cheered, "This is it! This is what kindness is!"

When they pulled up to school the next morning,
her dad placed a small *Be Kind* sticker on her shirt.
Kenzie smiled as she read it. "Good luck today, Kenz,"
he said as he gave her a hug goodbye. "I am proud of you."
Filled with excitement, she raced to her classroom.

be
Be Kind
kindness.
Kindness is

Be Kind.
Kindness
Is

One by one, each of her friends shared what kindness meant to them. Then it was Kenzie's turn. She eagerly stood up in front of her class and began reading...

"Kindness is love. For me, it's the way my parents tuck me in at night. The way my grandma sings in the car with me."

my girl
LOVE

love.
empathy.
compassion.
inclusion.
justice.
kindness.
justice.
kindness.
ALL are
WELCOME
here

"Kindness is empathy. It is feeling for others. My parents always say, 'It doesn't have to happen to you for it to matter to you.'"

"Kindness is compassion. It's the way my friend Angel held my hand when my pet goldfish died."

Be Kind
love.
empathy.
compassion.
inclusion.
justice.
kindness.

Be Kind
Inclusion

"Kindness is inclusion. It's making sure everyone feels safe and loved. It's the way you all invited me to play yesterday."

"Kindness is justice. It is using our voices to stand up for our friends. To do what is right."

Your vote matters
Vote

Mr. Warner smiled his biggest smile while Kenzie's classmates applauded her beautiful definitions of kindness.
Be Kind.
Kindness
is
Compassion
Justice
Love
Inclusion
Empathy

While the class was gone for lunch, Mr. Warner took Kenzie's words and made a song.
He shared it with them upon their return.

Kindness is *love.*
It's a hug from a friend.
Kindness is **empathy.**
It's an ear to lend.
Kindness is **compassion.**
It's a helping hand.
Kindness is **justice.**
It's seeking to understand.
This is **kindness.** Try it out.
This is kindness.
It's what *life's* about.

Be Kind.
love.
empathy.
compassion.
inclusion.
justice.
kindness.

Spread
True
Kindness

Kaitlin Johnstone is a former kindergarten teacher turned entrepreneur. She, along with her partner Kevin, started Kind Cotton, a clothing company dedicated to spreading true kindness while providing books to kids. They have a goal of donating a million inclusive books.

Follow them on social media:

Instagram & TikTok: @kindcotton
Facebook: @kindcottonclothing

Felicity LeFevre has been an elementary school teacher for 19 years and uses her time outside the classroom to illustrate and create teacher resources. *Kindness Is* is the second children's book she has illustrated. Born and raised in New York City, she now lives in the South with the three youngest of her six children.

Follow her on Instagram:
@palettebyfelicity

www.kindcotton.com